TO ELIZABETH

Library of Congress Cataloging-in-Publication Data Available
ISBN 978-0-545-24935-5

10 9 8 7 6 5 4 3 2 1   11 12 13 14 15

Printed in Singapore   46
First edition, May 2011

The display type was set in Circus Mouse.
The text was set in Linotype Conrad.
The art was created using acrylic paints.
Book design by Whitney Lyle

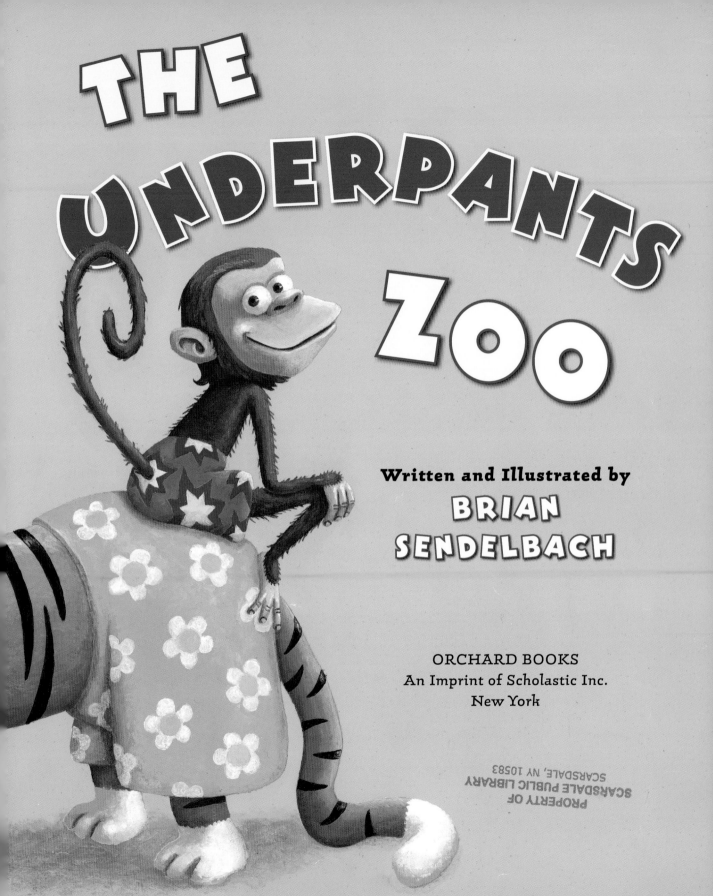

THE UNDERPANTS ZOO

Written and Illustrated by

BRIAN SENDELBACH

ORCHARD BOOKS
An Imprint of Scholastic Inc.
New York

There's a new zoo in town,
and here's what I've heard —
**THE
UNDERPANTS
ZOO**
is completely absurd. . . .

Come in and find out
why there's been such a fuss.
It's a zoo where the animals
wear underpants . . . just like us!

THE UNDERPANTS ZOO

It's important for **LION'S**
to appear royal and grand.

CAMEL says, "Mine keep getting filled up with sand!"

ZEBRAS have stripes,
but they like stars the best.

LEOPARD prefers spots,
as you may have guessed.

HIPPO'S have hearts,
because she's such a romantic.

ELEPHANT'S size is
Extra-Jumbo Gigantic.

KANGAROO'S boxers
need plenty of bounce.

For the sleepy **SLOTHS**,
it's comfort that counts.

The **SNAKES** are good friends,
so they share the same pair.

Make fun of **CROCODILE'S** style . . .
if you dare!

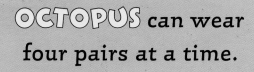

OCTOPUS can wear
four pairs at a time.

DOLPHINS in long johns?
It boggles the mind!

The **PENGUINS** chill their
underpants in the freezer. . . .

The MONKEYS' wild trunks
are always crowd-pleasers!

It may look as though **ANTEATER**
is doing some silly dance,
but look closely and you'll see —
HIS UNDERPANTS HAVE GOT ANTS!

The Underpants Zoo
(I am sorry to say)
is closing its gates
for the rest of the day.

But we'll visit again!
We'll drop by very soon.
Next time we'll stay
for the whole afternoon.

THE UNDERPANTS ZOO

CLOSED FOR
UNDERPANTS
DE-ANTSING